MR BLUE
in
Rainbow Planet

A Story Of Staying True To Who You Are

Dedicated to
H D D J M and to all the children of the world.
A special thanks to my daughter Hana,
for inspiring me to write this book.

Shine bright, be brave and the best you can be even in difficult times.

Maryam Yousaf
Illustrated by **Sheeba Shaikh**

On Rainbow Planet there once lived a Mr Blue.

Mr Blue was kind to everyone.

He loved to help others - even those of colours
different from his own.

Mr Blue visited the Greens when they were sick.

He gave charity to help the poor Yellows.

He shared food with his Orange neighbours.

And he helped the elderly Violets cross the road.

FOOD BANK

Mr Blue volunteered at his local food bank, and looked after the homeless.

If he saw something harmful in someone's way he removed it.

Mr Blue always thought
of ways to do some good
and tried his best to do them.

He spread the message
of peace to every colour he met,
speaking a kind word here and
another one there.

Every day, Mr Blue would read
the Big Book of Blues – the book on how
to be the best Blue ever.

And every night, just before bedtime, he would say a beautiful prayer for himself and for every colour on Rainbow Planet too.

When different colours
on Rainbow Planet
fought with each other,

... Mr Blue made
peace between them.

And whenever there was an emergency,
he rushed to help.

One day while Mr Blue was praying late at night,
he noticed a fire in the building next to his house.
He immediately woke everybody up and rang the fire brigade.

That day, Mr Blue helped save many lives.

Mr Blue had become the hero for every colour on Rainbow Planet.

His superpower was his wonderful, kind character.

No matter the colour of another Mr or Mrs,
Mr Blue always went out of his way to help them.

To him, that was exactly what being Blue meant.

Then one day something awful happened. Many Violets, Greens, Yellows and even Blues were harmed.

It was all over the news.
The media said that the damage was
caused by another Mr who was Blue.

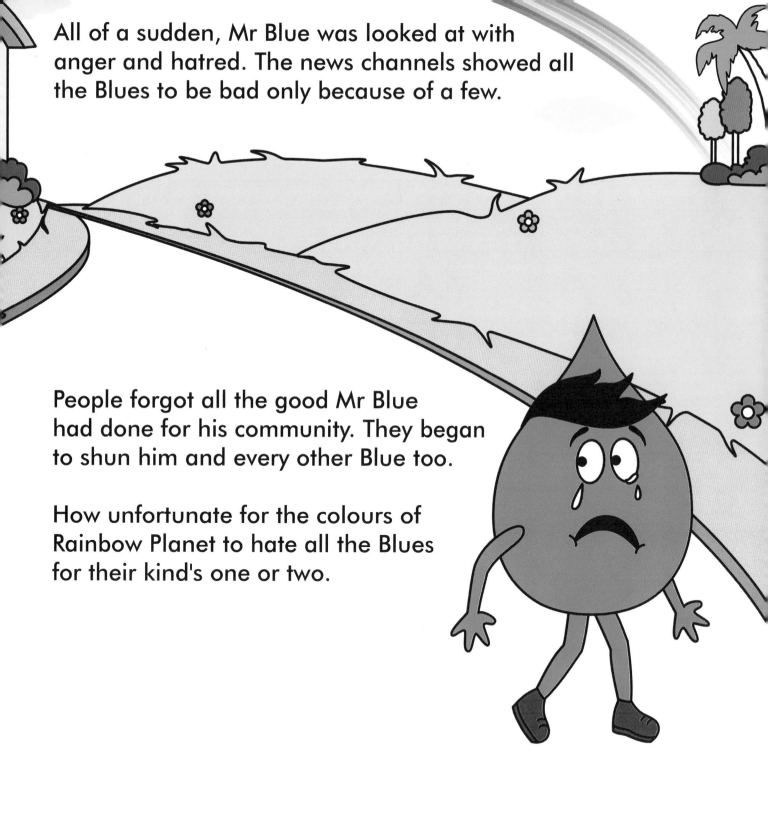

All of a sudden, Mr Blue was looked at with anger and hatred. The news channels showed all the Blues to be bad only because of a few.

People forgot all the good Mr Blue had done for his community. They began to shun him and every other Blue too.

How unfortunate for the colours of Rainbow Planet to hate all the Blues for their kind's one or two.

Everybody started to blame the Big Book of Blues.
They said, "This must be a bad book. It teaches no good."

But that was just not true.

The truth was that the Big Book of Blues
taught only what was good.

There were many Blues who remained true to it,
who followed its teachings, and were good and kind – just like
our Mr Blue. But there were also a few bad Blues
that disobeyed the Book's rules.

Sadly, the media of Rainbow Planet made its people believe that the millions of Blues that lived on Rainbow Planet were the same as these few.

The Blues went through blue times.
They were unfairly treated just because
they were Blue.

They were judged by the actions of Blues they never even knew.

And whenever a Blue out of a million Blues did one bad thing, all the Blues were expected to apologise even though they had nothing to do with it.

Hard as it was, the Blues didn't give up.
They held on tight to their Big Book of Blues and followed it
closely, so that they could keep being the best Blues of all.

With renewed faith in Rainbow Planet, the Blues continued to be patient and loving. They continued to pray for peace, and for every kind of colour there was.

They believed that there will come a day when all the colours of Rainbow Planet will see how the media is portraying a wrong picture of their kind.

And on that day, they will once again live together in colourful harmony.

IMPORTANT LESSONS

✓ The media we see today don't always give us the truth. They need to sell their stories to make money and news. So although they know the truth deep down, they continue to scare people for their own benefit.

✓ Be brilliantly kind and remember not to believe all that you hear until you check its facts, and research its realities.

✓ Judge people for who they are and what they do, not for the colour of their skin, their beliefs, or the country they live in.

✓ There are good actions and bad; the actions belong to the individual, and nothing else.

- ✓ Just as one bad Blue does not represent the rest of the million good Blues, a few bad people in the world do NOT represent the community or faith that they belong to.

- ✓ Remember: it's unfair and cruel to blame the evil actions of a few on those who look the same as, or are of the same beliefs or communities as them.

- ✓ Behave towards people the way you would like them to behave towards you.

- ✓ Always be kind and always be true to your own kind of blue.

- ✓ With patience, hope and prayer, you will get through!

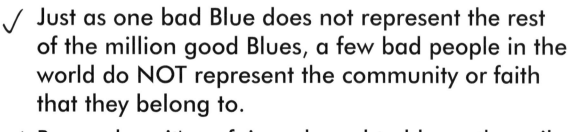

ACTIVITY

What did you learn from Mr Blue's story?

_____

_____

What do you think about the actions of the media
mentioned in the story?

_____

_____

Is it acceptable to blame an entire race or community
for the bad actions of a few among them? How would
you feel if you were blamed this way?

_____

_____

What was your favourite part of the story?

_____

_____

Draw and colour a picture of Mr Blue and Rainbow Planet.

GLOSSARY

Enrage: anger, inflame, madden.

Harmony: a situation in which people get along together.

Portray: to describe (someone or something) in a particular way.

Renew: give fresh life or strength to.

Shun: to ignore or reject (someone or something).

Unfortunate: unsuccessful, unlucky.

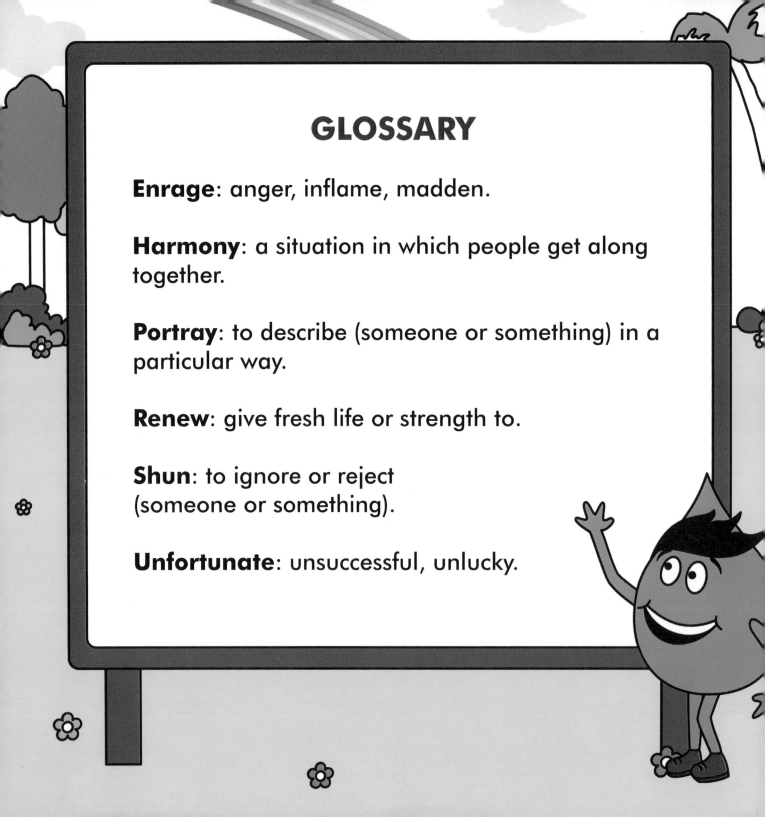

First published in 2018 by **Muslima Today Kids**
www.muslimatoday.com

Edited by
Umm Marwan Ibrahim

Text and illustrations copyright © by Maryam Yousaf

Muslima Today
www.muslimatoday.com
ISBN 978-0-9934078-6-4

Made in the USA
Columbia, SC
09 April 2018